BOOK ANALYSIS

Written by Cécile Perrel
Translated by Carly Probert

The Kite Runner

BY KHALED HOSSEINI

BrightSummaries.com

KHALED HOSSEINI

AFGHAN-BORN AMERICAN WRITER

- **Born in Kabul (Afghanistan) in 1965**
- **Notable works:**
  - *The Kite Runner* (2003), novel
  - *A Thousand Splendid Suns* (2007), novel

Khaled Hosseini is an Afghan-born American writer, born in Kabul in 1965. The son of a diplomat and a teacher, he left Afghanistan when he was very young, following his father in his various assignments. The family then lived in Paris, before requesting asylum in the United States, preferring not to return home while the country was under Russian control.

After obtaining his baccalaureate, Khaled Hosseini obtained a degree in biology and a doctorate in medicine. He has practiced as a doctor whilst writing novels ever since. His first book, *The Kite Runner* (2003), achieved considerable success, as did his second, *A Thousand Splendid Suns* (2007).

THE KITE RUNNER

THE STORY OF AFGHANISTAN FROM A CHILD'S PERSPECTIVE

- **Genre:** novel
- **Reference edition:** Hosseini, K. (2004) *The Kite Runner*. New York: Riverhead.
- **First edition:** 2003
- **Themes:** memories, racism, cowardice, guilt, forgiveness

The Kite Runner, a novel published in the United States in 2003, recounts Amir's exploration of his childhood memories, when he still lived in his country, Afghanistan, which he had to leave with his father to escape the Russian occupation. He leaves his world, his memories and his mistakes behind. However, they all come back to haunt him and he will find a way to redeem them.

This novel, which was a huge success, presents us with the history of Afghanistan in the 1970s, with the Russian occupation and the Taliban regime, as seen through the eyes of a child.

SUMMARY

LIKE TWO BROTHERS

Amir is a young Afghan boy of about ten years old. He lives alone with his father, Baba, who is one of the richest merchants in Kabul. Despite the unconditional love he devotes to Baba, their relationship is complicated. Indeed, Amir is the complete opposite of his father: he is rather puny, poor at sport, mostly interested in reading and allows himself to be heckled by other children. Suffering from this situation, he regularly finds refuge with Rahim, Baba's business partner. Rahim understands what is separating the father and son and tries to console the boy. He is also the only one who believes in Amir's writing talents.

Amir spends his days in the company of Hassan, the son of their servant, Ali, who belongs to the Hazaras. These people were persecuted by the Pashtuns for many years and, since then, Hassan and his father have been forced to work as servants. The two children are both missing the same thing: neither of them knew their mother. Amir's mother died during childbirth, while Hassan's fled shortly after he was born. They both had the same wet nurse and have always lived near to each other. Therefore, the links between them are strong. But the similarities do not stop there as they are, in fact, half-brothers, which Amir does not discover until he is an adult.

One evening in July 1973, after the king had been overthrown, shootings break out almost everywhere in Kabul, marking "the beginning of the end" for Amir. The next day, Amir and Hassan play in a wasteland and meet other boys their age who they know well. Among them is Assef, a violent and racist youth who worships Hitler. He hates the Hazaras and would like his country to be only populated by Pashtuns. As he prepares to hit Amir as punishment for being friends with Hassan, the latter takes out his slingshot and threatens him. Panicked, Assef leaves the scene, promising to avenge this insult.

KITE BATTLES

Each winter the traditional kite battles take place: each child arms himself with a kite and must attempt to cut the string of their competitors with the glass shards attached to their own kite. The last child standing is declared the winner and, in order to validate his victory, each kite eliminated must be collected by the winner. Amir and Hassan are particularly adept at this game: Amir handles the kite while Hassan looks for those that have fallen. This year, Amir is particularly keen to be the winner of the tournament in order to be closer to his father and make him proud.

The boy manages to win the various duels and, while he organizes his equipment, Hassan goes in search of the last kite beaten. After a while, Amir finds that his friend has been gone a long time and goes looking for him. He finds Hassan being ambushed by Assef and his friends. Assef orders Hassan to give him the kite and when he refuses, he decides to teach him and lesson and rapes him. Petrified and not daring to intervene, Amir watches the scene hidden behind a fence, before fleeing in horror from what he has just seen and from his own cowardice.

This event marks the end of their friendship. Subsequently, the two boys barely talk to one another anymore. Amir cannot stand the sight of Hassan, who reminds him of his cowardice. Therefore, he decides to get rid of Ali and his son by accusing them of theft. He gets his way and, despite the desperation of Baba, the two Hazaras leave their life.

REDEMPTION OF SINS

In March 1981, Amir flees Afghanistan with his father to escape the Russian occupation. They reach the United States and settle in California. There, his father works as a service station attendant, which completely changes their lifestyle. Meanwhile, Amir continues his studies and begins university where he studies writing techniques in order to become a writer, to the chagrin of his father who would have preferred him to become a lawyer or doctor. In 1989, he publishes his first novel.

One day, he meets Soraya Taheri, the daughter of the Afghan general. He immediately falls in love, proposes to her and marries her. A shadow nonetheless persists on the scene: they cannot have children. Amir believes that this is punishment for the cowardice he demonstrated as a child. But one day in June 2001, the phone rings: it is Rahim, his father's former business partner, who tells him that "there is a way to redeem [himself]". In fact, Rahim has a mission for him that involves saving the son of his old friend Hassan and raising him.

Amir agrees to visit him in Pakistan. Rahim then hands him a letter from Hassan, in which he tells Amir about his life: he explains that he is married, he has a son and that he hopes to see Amir again one day, to whom he gives his eternal devotion. However, Rahim does not tell him the next part of the story: Hassan and his wife were killed by the Taliban, leaving their son, Sohrab, orphaned. It is to save him from the orphanage that Rahim asked Amir to come. He also teaches Amir that Hassan was actually Baba's son, after he had a brief affair with his servant's wife.

Amir accepts the mission. He sees it as an opportunity to redeem himself and erase the harm he once caused his friend. Thus, he leaves for Kabul and discovers at the orphanage that the young Sohrab was taken away by a Taliban several weeks ago. When Amir finds him, he discovers with amazement that the Taliban who took him was Assef. The two men fight and Amir manages to get away with the child.

They both return to the United States where Soraya is delighted to welcome her husband's nephew. But the road will be long for Sohrab who, scarred by his experiences, retreats into a deep silence, refusing practically any attempt at communication. Amir is not discouraged and does everything in his power to provide a comfortable and reassuring life for his friend's son.

CHARACTER STUDY

AMIR

Amir is a young boy of ten years at the beginning of the story. Motherless, he lives in an exclusively male universe, surrounded by his father, Baba, Ali, the servant, and Hassan, Ali's son, who is one year younger than him and his playmate. Amir loves his father unconditionally, yet their relationship is still difficult. Indeed, Baba wishes that his son was more sporty and dynamic, while Amir is fearful, timid and quiet, and loves reading.

With Hassan, with whom he spends a lot of time, Amir's character changes completely: he becomes authoritarian and cynical, sometimes bordering on wickedness, and is desperate to test his friend's loyalty. It is his cowardice in the face of other children that destroys his world as he does not dare to react to Hassan's aggression. Out of cowardice, he prefers to run away and pretend he doesn't know what happened. He prefers to drive Hassan and his father away on a false pretext, rather than see his friend every day, whose face reminds him of his own cowardice.

Later, Amir finally dares to oppose his father when it comes to choosing his field of study: he wants to become a writer, not a doctor or a lawyer. But it is the call from Rahim and his return home that truly change him. His attitude during Hassan's rape has weighed on his conscience for decades and he finally has a chance, not to redeem himself – as the damage has already been done and cannot be repaired –, but to put his fears aside and prove himself to be altruistic. The act is especially important as it involves the son of Hassan.

Amir is not a conventional hero, since he is a cowardly and selfish character. However, he represents our own fears and allows the reader to ask: "What would I have done in his situation? Would I have intervened to save my friend, at the risk of putting my life in danger or would I also have chosen to run away?"

BABA

"My father was a force of nature, a towering Pashtun specimen with a thick beard, a wayward crop of curly brown hair as unruly as the man himself, hands that looked capable of uprooting a willow tree, and a black glare that would 'drop the devil to his knees begging for mercy'" (Chapter 3), Amir explains.

Widowed, he never remarries, though at the end of the novel we learn that he had a brief affair with Ali's wife and that Hassan is his son. A rich merchant, he owns two pharmacies, a restaurant and exports carpets. He can give his son a life free from want, but he seems unable to offer him affection. Baba does not understand Amir, he does not share his interests and it upsets him to see Amir so unsure of himself. While he is overbearing in Afghanistan, he finds himself in a position of inferiority when he moves to the United States: he no longer feels at home, has lost his bearings and Amir then takes the lead.

HASSAN

Hassan is officially Ali's son, the servant of the house. Belonging to the Hazara tribe, he is condemned by birth to be a servant and have no education. Nevertheless, he is lively and intelligent, and loves Amir unconditionally. He shares all of his games and is ready to sacrifice himself for him, since he is the one who puts Assef in disarray during their first altercation, an attitude that will determine his fate since Assef will later get his revenge. He knows that Amir was present during his rape and that his friend lied about their alleged theft in order to get rid of him, but he doesn't reveal anything: his dedication is boundless.

Before his death, he leaves a letter for Amir in which he assures him of his loyalty. Far from being a boy without character, Hassan thus appears as both generous and faithful.

ANALYSIS

THE FATHER FIGURE

The Kite Runner is an almost exclusively male novel. Indeed, women do not appear very often, with the exception of Soraya and her mother in the second part of the book. The image of men, particularly of the father, is thus important.

In the novel, we can find different types of fathers: the adored yet distant father embodied by Baba; the ideal father in the character of Rahim; the discreet father who would do anything for his son, such as Ali; and finally, the man who wants to become a father but cannot.

- Baba is the only parent known by Amir since the death of his mother during childbirth. Yet, they both have a difficult relationship. Amir speaks of him as follows: "Baba and I lived in the same house, but in different spheres of existence" (Chapter 6). These two people do not understand each other: Amir is convinced that his father holds it against him that he "killed" his mother, and Baba does not support his son's modest and timid character. His physical weakness seems to him to be a defect and he finds Amir's repeated spells of sickness in the car insufferable. However, Amir says: "I worshiped Baba with an intensity approaching the religious" (Chapter 4). The only time the two are united is in Amir's victory in the kite tournament. But this comes at a price, as Amir had to sacrifice Hassan for this. Hassan is, in fact, Baba's secret son, which we learn, like Amir, at the end of the novel. We finally realize why Baba had always treated Hassan like his own son, which sometimes surprised Amir.

- Ali, Hassan's official father, is discreet, but just and devoted to his son. He does not take part in any of Hassan's activities. However, he does not hesitate to support Hassan when he is accused of theft by Amir.
- Rahim is the friend and business partner of Baba, and the only adult man who pays attention to Amir, who believes in him and his qualities. In this sense, he is the ideal father figure. When the relationship between Baba and Amir is too difficult, Amir comes to also wish that Rahim were his father. It is Rahim who first encourages Amir in his writing projects, and also reminds him of his duties and asks him to redeem his sins by returning to Afghanistan to save Sohrab.
- Amir, as an adult, in turn wants more than anything to become a father and yet, his is unable to have children in his marriage to Soraya: "Perhaps something, someone, somewhere, had decided to deny me fatherhood for the things I had done. Maybe this was my punishment, and perhaps justly so" (Chapter 13). Later, when collecting Sohrab, he must work to gain his trust. Amir has to learn to be a father and to give in to his child's reluctance so as not to rush the process.

THEME OF GUILT

Guilt designates a feeling that leads one to consider oneself responsible for an event. Amir feels this throughout the novel, for several reasons:

- He feels guilty for the death of his mother. Indeed, as she died giving birth to him, he imagines that he is liable, even though, of course, he is not;
- Thereafter, he feels guilty for the attack on Hassan, and this is a memory that he will carry with him for the rest of his life. Amir attended the scene, he could have intervened to defend his friend, but all he wanted to do was bring the kite to his father and to finally see pride in his eyes. It is for this reason that he prefers to flee. Yet, the guilt he feels for his own cowardice soon becomes intolerable. The mere sight of Hassan makes him recall his cowardice and weakness. Only his departure for the United States, allowing him to get away from the place of his mistake, relieves him: "For me, America was a place to bury my memories" (Chapter 11).

Baba is also prey to guilty feelings, even though we discover this at the end of the novel, when the truth of Hassan's birth is revealed to Amir. Baba is his real father. He feels guilty for not being able to take care of him as he does Amir. Thus, he takes every opportunity to try and redeem his mistake through gifts, like the cosmetic operation to cure the child's cleft lip he gives to Hassan for his birthday.

Guilt is one of the most important themes in the novel. The author shows us how the characters succeed or fail at living with this feeling. Throughout his life, Baba has wanted to make amends, while Amir preferred to avoid his feelings for much of his existence before finally expressing them. From that moment on, he takes responsibility and tries as much as he can to repair his mistakes.

COMING-OF-AGE STORY

The genre of the coming-of-age story, also called the novel of education, was born in Germany in the eighteenth century under the name Bildungsroman. It recounts the path and the evolution of a hero, who at the beginning of the work is young and inexperienced. Thus, we see them mature, evolve, test their mettle and form their own view of life. In this type of structure, the character must face different events that, ultimately, provide them with wisdom. The coming-of-age story therefore describes the maturation of the hero.

Amir follows a path which makes him the hero of a coming-of-age story. His childhood was golden, protected from the vicissitudes of life, and he is guided by a certain morality. Ali, speaking of the two children brought up by the same wet nurse, says that "there was a brotherhood between people who had fed from the same breast, a kinship that not even time could break" (Chapter 2). But Amir quickly realizes that he lives in a world of inequality: he is a Pashtun and lives in a beautiful house, while his friend Hassan and his father, who are almost part of the family, live in a miserable hut in the garden, just because they are Hazaras. This feeling is reinforced by the words of Assef, who hates the Hazara people, claiming that Afghanistan belongs to the Pashtuns.

Later, when Hassan is attacked, Amir realizes that this act may go unpunished because it was committed by a Pashtun against a Hazara. And yet, the boy cannot bring himself to accept this fatality, despite his own cowardice that allowed the crime to happen. Amir suddenly feels, through this drama, that life is not the way he had pictured it before. Living in a privileged world he knew neither violence nor vice. He suddenly discovers something that leaves an indelible trace. After first trying to escape his responsibilities, Amir only truly becomes a man after having faced reality, i.e. after redeeming his actions against his former friend by raising his son.

Amir's education also depends on the geographic territory. As long as he is in Afghanistan, he remains under the control of his father who makes all of his decisions for him. However, things change completely when they leave to settle in California. There, Baba loses his bearings, allowing Amir to gain his own. In his own country, Baba was a strong man, the decision maker: here, it is Amir who makes the decisions and becomes the driving force behind his own life. He finally manages to build himself and escape the yoke of his father (even if he only wanted the best for his son).

Amir truly completes his journey during his return home to save Sohrab. The circle is then completed. Amir grows up through the decisions he must make to continue living at peace with himself: after he did nothing to rescue Hassan, he must now act to save the son of his old friend.

A PICTURE OF AFGHANISTAN

Throughout the novel, the author provides us with information on Afghanistan, which saw a particularly unstable political regime for many years.

A central Asian country, formerly a hotspot on the Silk Road,

Afghanistan suffered from a deep political imbalance from 1919. However, the novel does not go so far back in time and begins in the 1970s, during the reign of Mohammed Zaher Chah. The country was prosperous up until the night of 17 July 1973, when the king was overthrown by Mohammed Daoud Khan and the Republic was proclaimed. "Afghanistan changed forever" (Chapter 4) Amir says of this episode. Indeed, it is from that time onwards that Russia strengthens its grip on the country, reaching its peak in 1978 with the overthrow of Daoud in a coup d'état supported by the Russians. It is this Russian occupation that pushes Amir and his father to flee their country "You couldn't trust anyone in Kabul anymore – for a fee or under threat, people told on each other, neighbor on neighbor, child on parent, brother on brother, servant on master, friend on friend" (Chapter 10).

When Amir and Baba are living in California, it is the Taliban who take power in Afghanistan. This is a situation that has always frightened Baba, who tells Amir: "God help us all if Afghanistan ever falls into their hands" (Chapter 3). The Taliban advocate the Islamization of society, morals and justice. Only divine law matters. When Amir returns to Afghanistan, he is horrified to see the state of his country and Kabul, which bears the scars of many years of war. In the city, the Taliban are constantly circulating to monitor the population. He even attends a stoning for adultery, against his intentions. He also recognizes the Taliban man who is executing the sentence: it is none other than Assef, who is also holding Sohrab prisoner. Thus, throughout the novel, the reader follows the political evolution of the country.

FURTHER REFLECTION

SOME QUESTIONS TO THINK ABOUT...

- What image of family is proposed by the novel?
- "If there's a God out there, then I would hope he has more important things to attend to than my drinking scotch or eating pork." What is Baba referring to here? Develop your answer.
- What is the image of women conveyed by the characters of Soraya and her mother?
- How is religion presented in this novel? Develop your answer.
- What other contemporary novels can *The Kite Runner* be compared with? Explain your answer.
- The story of the hero Amir cannot be completely separated from that of his country, Afghanistan. Explain how historical events influence the destiny of the character.
- Could we call *The Kite Runner* a historical novel? Explain your answer using the definition of the genre as well as specific examples from the novel.

We want to hear from you!
Leave a comment on your online library
and share your favourite books on social media!

FURTHER READING

REFERENCE EDITION

- Hosseini, K. (2004) *The Kite Runner*. New York: Riverhead.

www.brightsummaries.com

Ebook EAN: 9782806271143

Paperback EAN: 9782806271150

Legal Deposit: D/2015/12603/484

Cover: © Primento

Digital conception by Primento, the digital partner of publishers.

Printed in Germany
by Amazon Distribution
GmbH, Leipzig

18995484R00016